For Benjamin

First published in Great Britain in 1989
by Hutchinson Children's Books
An imprint of Century Hutchinson Ltd
Brookmount House, 62-65 Chandos Place,
Covent Garden, London WC2N 4NW

Century Hutchinson Australia (Pty) Ltd
88-91 Albion Street, Surry Hills, NSW 2010

Century Hutchinson New Zealand Ltd
32-34 View Road, PO Box 40-086, Glenfield, Auckland 10

Century Hutchinson South Africa (Pty) Ltd
PO Box 337, Bergvlei 2012, South Africa

Set in Futura Light

Printed and bound in Belgium
by Proost International Book Production

British Library Cataloguing in Publication Data

Cartwright, Ann
The last dodo.
I. Title   II. Cartwright, Reg
823'.914[J]

ISBN 0-09-172150-4

THE LAST
DODO

Ann and Reg Cartwright

HUTCHINSON

London Sydney Auckland Johannesburg

King Glut was a large, fat, greedy king who lived in a large damp, cold castle. Of all the things he liked to eat, his favourite food was eggs.

King Glut had a chef called Adrian. Poor Adrian! His life was a misery. He spent all day in the kitchen trying to think of new recipes to please the king. He served quail eggs, hens' eggs, duck eggs, goose eggs, and even swan eggs. He fried them, he scrambled them, he curried them and he boiled them; but the king was never satisfied. 'More! More!' he would cry. 'Can't you try something different.'

One morning at breakfast, King Glut read in his newspaper that a dodo's egg had been spotted on a distant island. 'A dodo's egg!' he cried, licking his fat lips. 'What a delicacy. I must have it.'

He ordered Adrian to prepare the boat. 'There's no time to lose,' he cried.

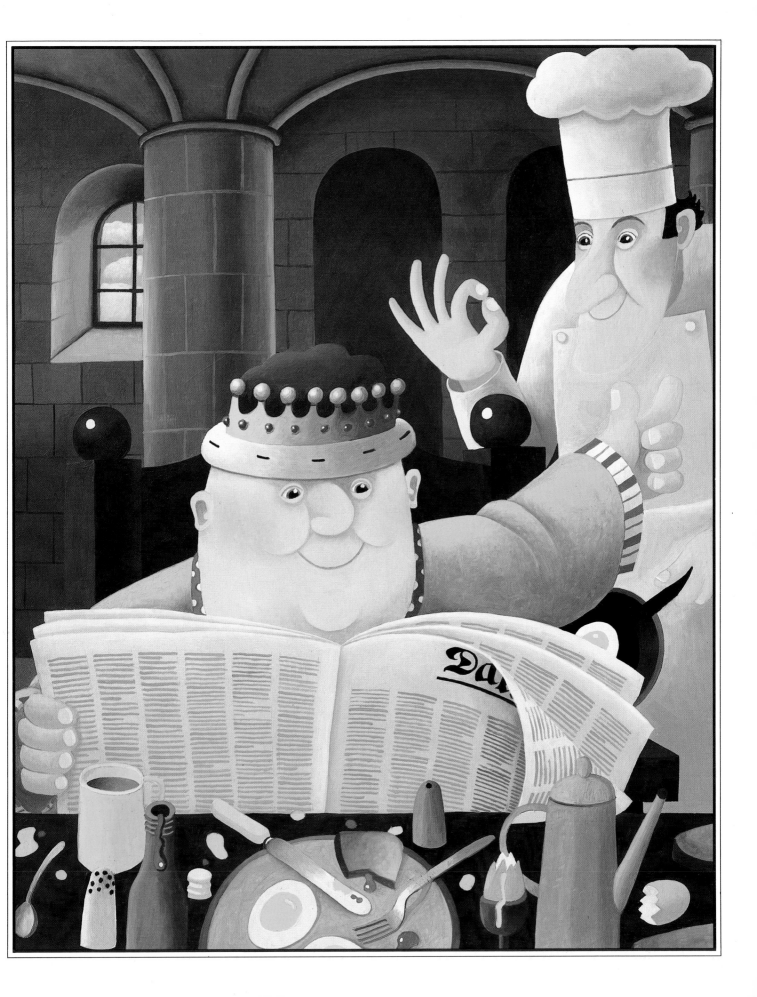

When the boat was ready, King Glut climbed aboard, clutching a giant egg cup and spoon in readiness for the great event.

'Row harder, Adrian,' he shouted. 'We must be first to reach the egg.'

For three days and nights they crossed
the ocean. One morning a great ship
appeared on the horizon. It was the
Green Dove.

'Ahoy there,' called the captain
through his loud-hailer. 'Where are you
bound with that egg cup? Not after the
dodo's egg, I hope. It's the last one in
the whole world and this ship is on a
mission to protect it.'

'Oh, no, I'm not egg bound,' lied the
king. 'And this? Why, it's no egg cup,
it's my crown!' And he turned it upside
down and put it on his head.

'Well, be careful,' warned the
captain. 'There are rough seas ahead.'

But the king took no notice. He was determined to find the egg and nothing was going to stop him. He should have listened, though, for the sky suddenly turned dark. The sea became so rough, and the waves so high, that Adrian could not control the boat.

'Help!' he shouted, as a mighty wave, as high as a house, crashed over the little boat and turned it upside down. King Glut and Adrian gasped and spluttered and hiccupped and swallowed great mouthfuls of salty water as they were carried away.
Up on top of the wave they went and down the other side.

Just as they were losing hope of being
saved they felt land beneath their feet.
King Glut rubbed his eyes. 'An island,'
he cried. 'We must be near the dodo's
egg.'

But the island began to move. . . .

It wasn't an island. It was an enormous whale!

A huge jet of water shot up into the air like a fountain. Then away the whale swam with King Glut and Adrian hanging on for dear life.

Even in this new danger, the king could not forget his greed. 'We'll *never* be the first now,' he spluttered, desperately hanging on to his cup and spoon.

For many hours the whale swam on.
Then, through the mist, came a sound.
Hoot! Hoot! Hoot! Hoot! It was the
Green Dove coming to the rescue.

'There she blows,' shouted the
captain, as he caught sight of the
whale.

The captain hauled the wet and
bedraggled pair on board. He kindly
gave them supper and laid their soggy
clothes out on deck to dry. Was the
king grateful? Not a bit of it. He was
congratulating himself on his good
fortune. Now he would be *sure* to find
the egg, with the good captain to
guide him to it.

Next morning, as the mist began to
clear, a small green island came into
view. 'This is our destination,' said the
captain. 'Here we will find the dodo's
egg.'

'Not if I get to it first,' the king
whispered to Adrian.

The captain moored his ship, and
King Glut and Adrian followed him on
to the beach. They found themselves in
a beautiful bay surrounded by tall trees.
'Follow me,' said the captain, as he
tiptoed into the undergrowth with King
Glut and Adrian close behind.

Soon the captain stopped. He parted
the leaves and there, nestled in the
warm sand, was a magnificent egg. A
dodo's egg. The very last one in the
whole wide world.

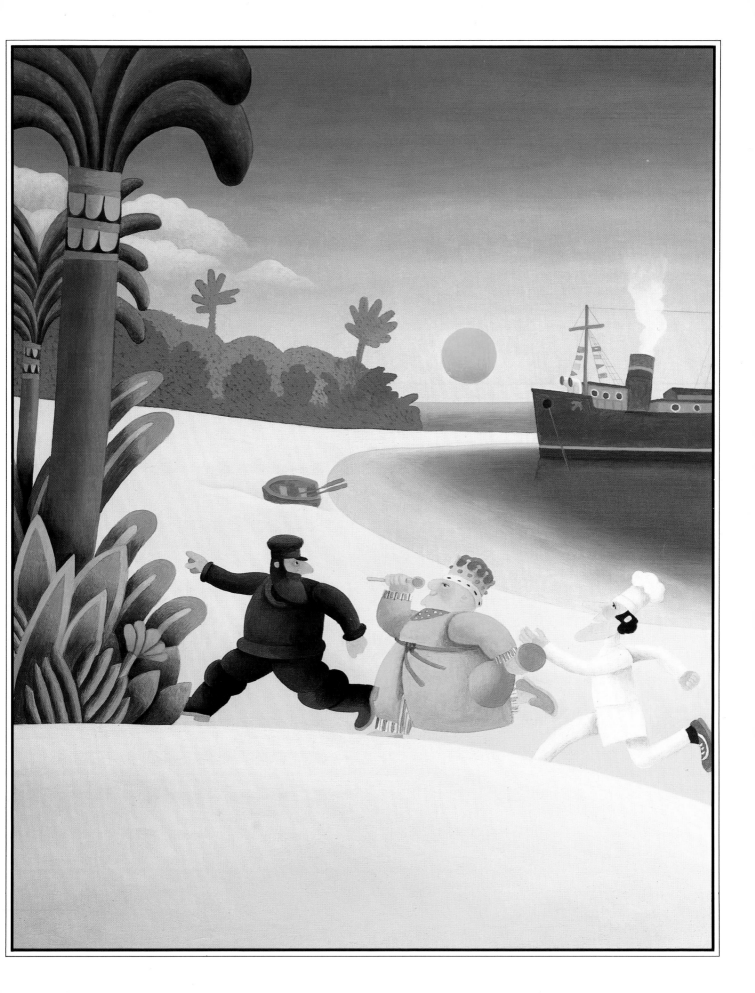

King Glut pushed the captain aside. 'Mine! Mine!' he cried, grabbing the egg. 'Quick Adrian, boil some water. I'll have it poached!'

But then something happened. There was a rustle, and a crackle, and a pecking sound. A crack appeared in the egg, then another, and another. Out of the egg popped a baby dodo. 'Cheep!' it said, as it looked at the world for the first time.

'Ahh,' said the captain.

'Ahh, ahh,' said Adrian.

Then there was silence. Adrian and the captain watched as the dodo gave the king a sharp peck on the nose.

'Ahh, ahh, ahhhhh!' sighed the king.

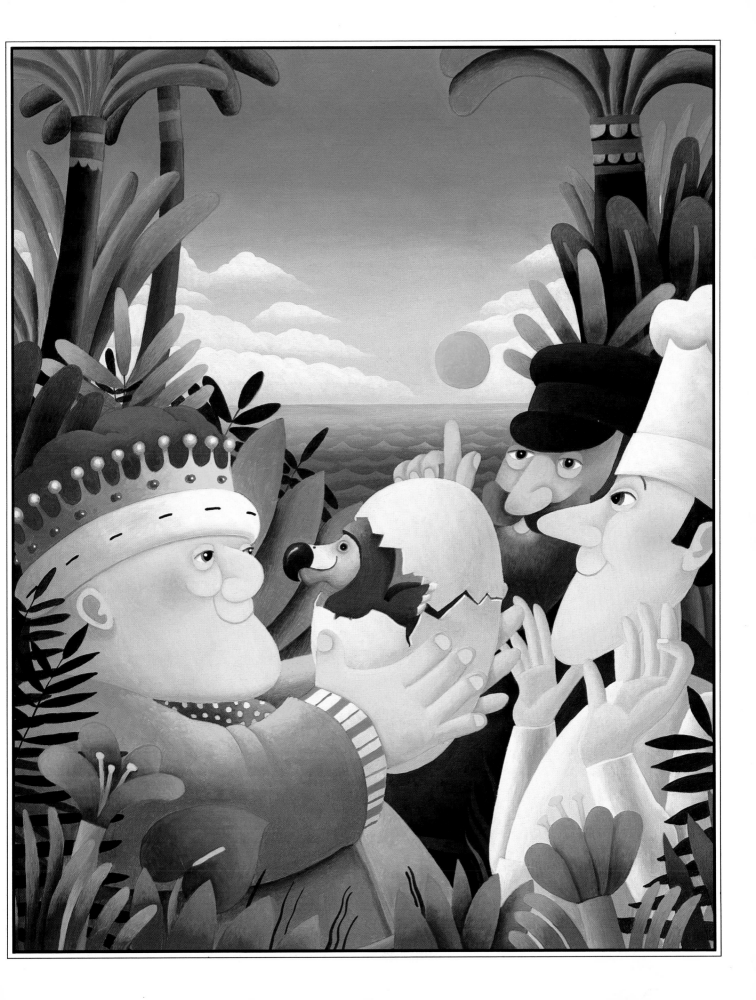

He was enchanted. He dropped his
egg cup and threw away his spoon.
'From this day on,' he declared, 'the
eating of eggs will be banned
throughout my whole kingdom.'
   'And from this day on,' added the
captain, 'the dodo will live in peace and
safety on this unknown island.'

Then the Green Dove sailed for home.
The king was true to his word. From that
day to this he has never eaten another
egg.

And the dodo? No one has ever found
the island.
Let's hope they never will!